Don't Be Bored, Dinosaurs!

'Don't Be Bored, Dinosaurs!'
An original concept by Elizabeth Dale
© Elizabeth Dale 2024

Illustrated by Lwillys Tafur

Published by MAVERICK ARTS PUBLISHING LTD
Suite 1, Hillreed House, 54 Queen Street,
Horsham, West Sussex, RH13 5AD
© Maverick Arts Publishing Limited August 2024
+44 (0)1403 256941

A CIP catalogue record for this book is available at the British Library.

ISBN 978-1-83511-029-4

Printed in India

www.maverickbooks.co.uk

London Borough of Enfield	
91200000823863	
Askews & Holts	25-Oct-2024
JF YGN BEGINNER READE	
ENBUSH	

Turquoise

This book is rated as: Turquoise Band (Guided Reading)

Don't Be Bored, Dinosaurs!

By Elizabeth Dale   Illustrated by Lwillys Tafur

Flicky yawned. It was a sleepy Monday afternoon at Dino School. Even worse, they were learning History. Boring! Who wanted to know about the first dinosaurs roaming the world? Yawn!

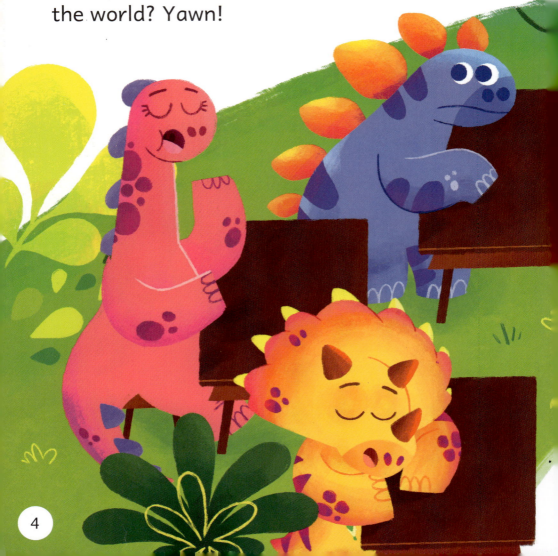

"Flicky!" cried Mr Megasnaurus. "Stop yawning! I do not want to see all the way down your long neck!"

"Sorry," she said. "I can't help it."

"History is boring," said Terry, yawning an even bigger yawn.

"We agree!" cried the other dinosaurs.

"Can't we study the future instead?" asked Flicky.

Mr Megasnaurus smiled. "Well, I shouldn't really..." he said, "but I could take you forward to the 21st century."

Everyone suddenly sat up.

"Very well," said Mr Megasnaurus.

"Come together. Hold on to each other.

Close your eyes."

Class D had never moved so fast.

Then, suddenly...

WHOOSH!

Flicky blinked. She couldn't believe her eyes. They'd arrived in the future! The animals here were so tiny.

"Hurry! Hide!" Mr Megasnaurus whispered.

"Nobody must know you're here!"

Everyone quickly hid.

This was hard as they were all so big!

"These are child animals at school,"

Mr Megasnaurus explained.

"They've got weird extra flappy skin!" Terry said.

"They're called clothes," said Mr Megasnaurus.

"They take them off at night."

'How strange!' thought Flicky.

The children were all chasing a ball. Instead of picking it up, they kicked it. But that was not the oddest thing. They absolutely loved it when the ball got stuck in a big net!

A whistle blew and the children ran inside. "Right," said Mr Megasnaurus. "Be back here in an hour to go home. Until then, enjoy exploring. Remember, stay out of sight and don't make a sound!"

It was difficult not making a sound when you had big dinosaur feet—and you were excited! As other dinosaurs ran elsewhere, Flicky crept up to see the children again. She peered through a window.

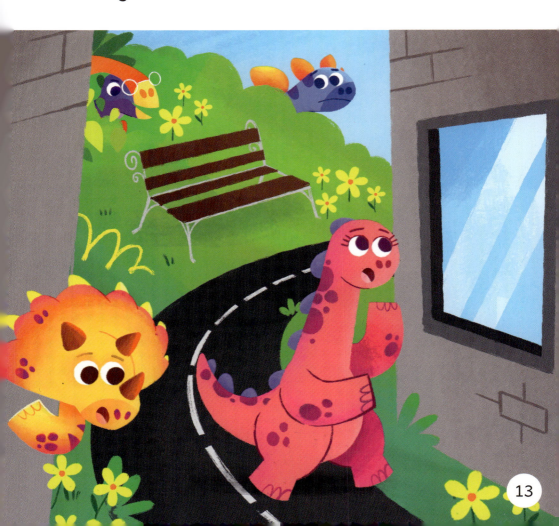

Every child was singing, "Two times two is four, two times three is six." What a boring song! How silly!

In another room, children were drawing funny lines on paper. They weren't even in colour!

Next door, everyone was staring at a big white screen. But it didn't have moving pictures, just strange squiggles. Flicky frowned. Boring again!

In another room, Flicky saw children with plates of stinky brown sludge and green balls. Then they put it in their mouths – and swallowed it! Disgusting!

One child gave up eating and looked towards Flicky.

Whoops! She quickly ducked out of sight—just in time, hopefully!

But then she saw the same child again.

He was running towards her, yelling,

"I can't believe it!"

"Shh! Nobody must hear us!" Flicky

hissed. "Follow me!"

"A dinosaur! You're a real-life dinosaur!" the child yelled.

"Shh! I know!" Flicky laughed. "What are you?"

"I'm Henry!" he said. "Can we play?"

"Yes!" said Flicky. She bent down her long neck and the Henry climbed on.

"Whee!" he yelled, as Flicky lifted her head. "I can see for miles!"

It seemed Henrys couldn't be quiet! Maybe they should hurry further away?

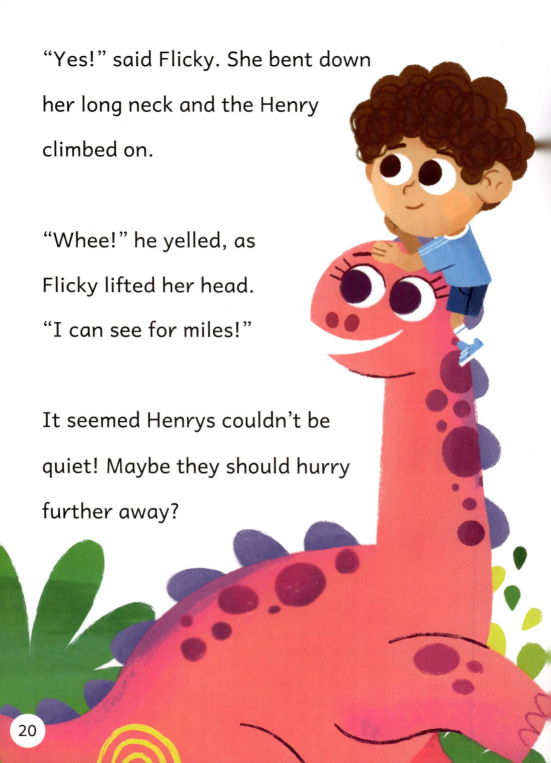

"Hold on!" Flicky said. And she ran as fast as the wind.

"Whee!" the Henry cried, even louder.

"This is fun!"

They slowed down when they reached some woods.

"Do you like school?" asked Flicky.

"Yeah, but it starts way too early," the Henry said. "Sometimes I don't have time for breakfast."

Flicky stopped so suddenly that the Henry slid off.

"Sorry," she said, lifting him back up. "That's unbelievable! Dino School doesn't start until lunchtime! I'm always in bed until then."

"I would be," said the Henry, "but Mum wakes me up." Flicky was so surprised, she walked into a tree. Boing! "Sorry?! Your mum wakes you up when you're asleep?" she asked, amazed.

"And she makes me go to bed when I'm wide awake!" moaned the Henry.

"Crazy!" said Flicky. "Poor you! You deserve some fun!" And she slid with the Henry down a grassy bank. Whee!

Then Flicky lifted him high into trees...

...and helped him slide back down along her neck. They had such fun.

Flicky was just swimming along a stream, giving the Henry a ride, when she saw Mr Megasnaurus and the other dinosaurs running towards her.

"Wow! So many amazing dinosaurs!" cried the Henry.

"Shh! Hide quick!" Flicky hissed. "I'm sorry, I have to go back now!"

"Oh no!" cried the Henry. "But I've had so much fun. Will I ever see you again?"

"Of course!" said Flicky. "I'll come back whenever I can, I promise. Make sure you look out for me!"

"You'll be hard to miss!" laughed the Henry. "Goodbye, Flicky! Thanks for all the fun!"

WHOOSH! The dinosaurs were back! And Mr Megasnaurus was droning on about History again.

But Flicky wasn't bored. She was happy— busy planning the fun she'd have with the Henry when she returned!

Quiz

1. What are the dinos learning at school?
a) English
b) Science
c) History

2. What does Flicky ask to study instead?
a) The future
b) Magic
c) Humans

3. What does Henry not like about school?
a) The school dinners
b) It starts too early
c) There's too much homework

4. What does Flicky walk into?
a) A house
b) A tree
c) A squirrel

5. Goodbye, Flicky! Thanks for all the…
a) fun!
b) work!
c) memories!

Turn over for answers   31

Book Bands for Guided Reading

The Institute of Education book banding system is a scale of colours that reflects the various levels of reading difficulty. The bands are assigned by taking into account the content, the language style, the layout and phonics. Word, phrase and sentence level work is also taken into consideration.

Maverick Early Readers are a bright, attractive range of books covering the pink to white bands. All of these books have been book banded for guided reading to the industry standard and edited by a leading educational consultant.

To view the whole Maverick Readers scheme, visit our website at www.maverickearlyreaders.com

Or scan the QR code above to view our scheme instantly!

Quiz Answers: 1c, 2a, 3b, 4b, 5a